ISBN: 978-1-8384003-2-3

A CIP catalogue record for this book is available from the British Library.

First published by Boz Publications Ltd 2021

Boz Publications Ltd.

71-75 Shelton Street, Covent Garden, London WC2H 9JQ

office@bozpublications.com - www.bozpublications.com

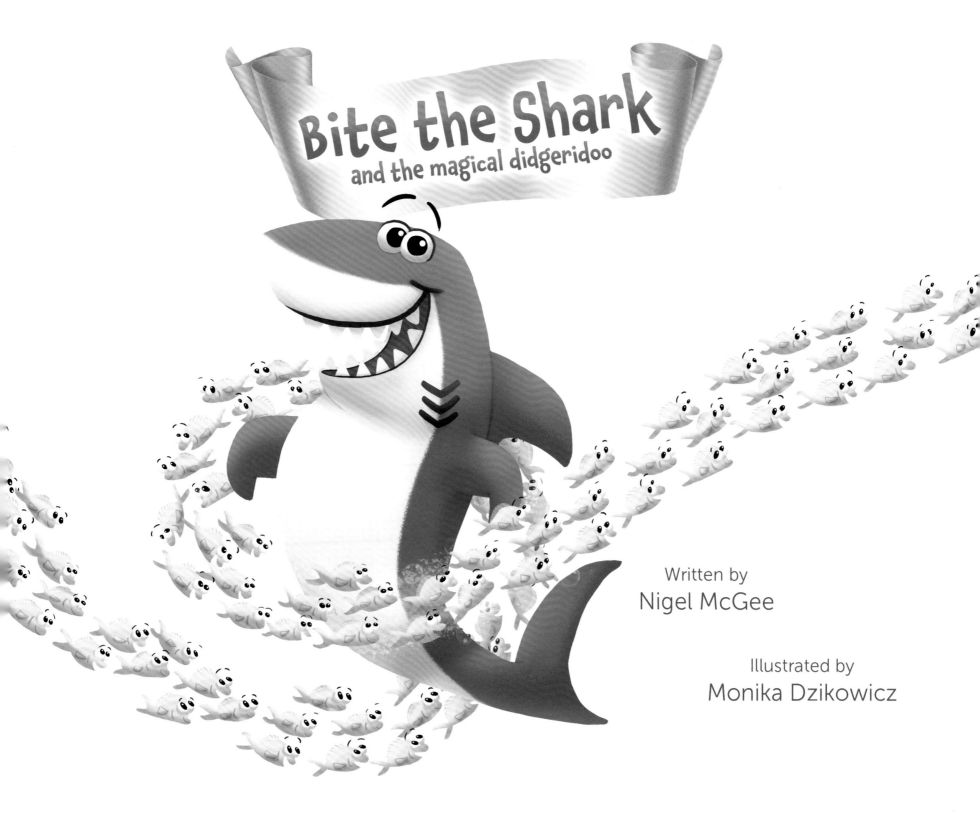

Bite the Shark
and the magical didgeridoo

Written by
Nigel McGee

Illustrated by
Monika Dzikowicz

This is Bite. Bite is a friendly, great white shark.
He loves to swim, play, explore and of course, **eat!**

But there is something about Bite
that makes him a little...**unusual.**

Unlike his other shark friends who are carn-i-vours because they eat meat, and pesc-a-tar-ian's because they eat seafood, Bite, only eats plants.

He is a **veg-e-tar-ian** shark.

Bite doesn't mind being different.
He loves how being a vegetarian makes him strong and healthy.

In fact, he is so strong and healthy that the mer-King and Queen made him

the guardian of Kingdom Underwatervania

(which is a big deal if you live underwater).

One night, while Underwatervania slept under the moon's shimmering reflection, the duty guard felt very strange and very, very, sleepy.
She tried **EVERYTHING** to stay awake.

First, she did star jumps.
That didn't work.

Next, swimming on the spot.
That didn't work.

She even gobbled down six coffee cockles
and drank two chocolate sea cucumber smoothies.
That didn't work either.

"I can't understand
why I feel so... so..."

The guard never got to finish the sentence,
falling into a deep and peaceful sleep.

Behind a nearby rock, a group of naughty
crocodiles giggled to themselves.

"Too easy".
"Good one, mate".
"Hehehe.
This magical didgeridoo
is amazing".

"Less of the chat",
said the crocodile boss.

"We still have work to do.
Next stop, the royal bedroom,
then the treasure room".

The naughty crocodiles crept into the underwater castle.
As quick as a hungry crocodile snaps its jaws around a juicy treat,
they bundled the mer-King and Queen into a large, smelly sack.
"Next stop. The jewels!"

They zoomed around the Jewel Room, grabbing gold, emeralds and pearls. Within seconds, the room was bare. Within minutes, they were heading back to their den, pleased with their prized catch of the day.

In their excitement, the crocodiles forgot to play the magical didgeridoo to the mer-King and Queen. They hadn't noticed that the quick-witted Queen had cut a little hole in the bag and dropped pearls from her necklace along the way.

She had left a trail for someone...
A SPECIAL SOMEONE... to follow.
Can you guess who that **SOMEONE** is?

The next morning, the Kingdom of Underwatervania was in chaos.
Not only did they have no jewels left to pay the water bill,
but the mer-King and Queen were **MISSING!**

Only one person to call.

"BITE!
WE NEED YOU!"

As if by super, vegetarian magic, Bite suddenly appeared. He examined the messy bedroom, noticing something strange and very smelly on the bed.

"Ahh Hah. A stinky fabric thread. **This is our first clue.** The robbers kidnapped our mer-King and Queen, putting them in a smelly sack".

Bite swam over to the treasure room, noticing another interesting thing.

"A cork hat. **This is our second clue.**
And I now know who did this - it's those **naughty crocodiles**".
The guards were shocked by the news, and slightly in awe of Bite's detective skills.
They made a mental note to themselves, 'we must eat more seaweed and less meat'.

Just then, Bite saw a trail of pearls leading out of the treasure room.

"**And this is our third clue.**
Our clever mer-King and Queen
have left a trail for us to follow.

But what I still don't understand
is how the crocodiles got into the castle
without our guards noticing".

He summoned his best team of guards -
The SAS (Special Aqua Service),
and as night fell upon the Kingdom, the rescue mission began.

Under the moonlight, Bite and the SAS tip-toed onto the beach wearing their special scuba breathing apparatus.

The naughty crocodiles were feasting and drinking, wearing all sorts of jewels and pearls.

Bite could see the mer-King and Queen
tied up by the campfire looking worried.
How would they rescue them?

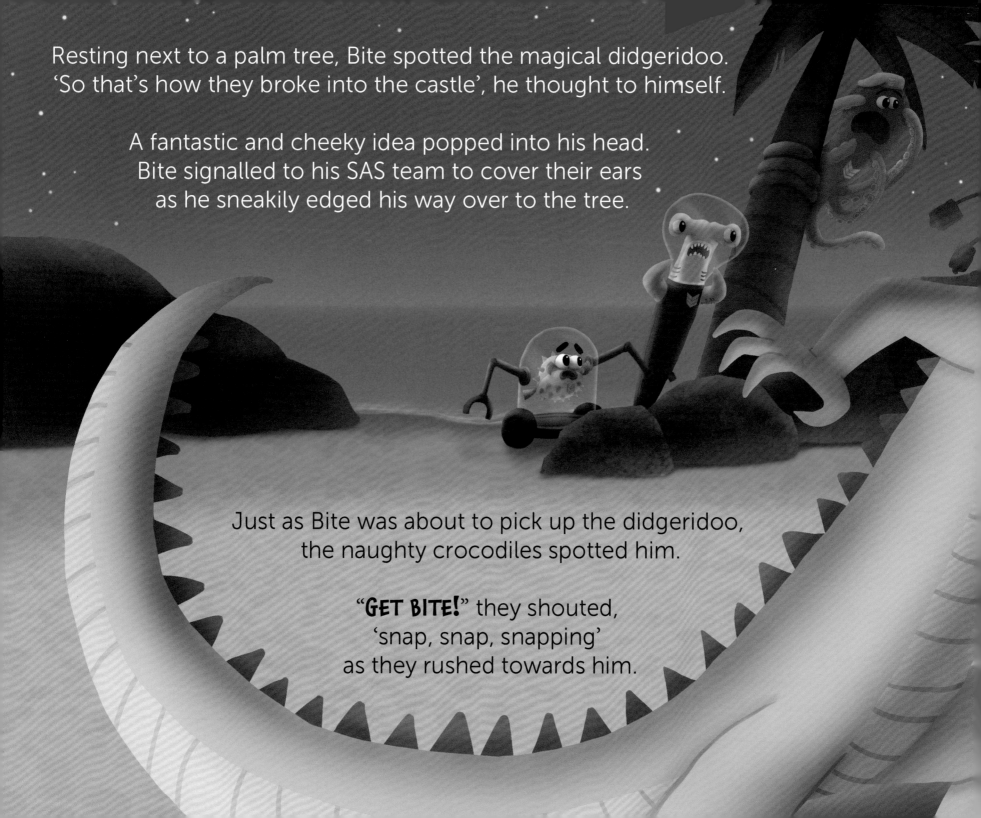

Resting next to a palm tree, Bite spotted the magical didgeridoo.
'So that's how they broke into the castle', he thought to himself.

A fantastic and cheeky idea popped into his head.
Bite signalled to his SAS team to cover their ears
as he sneakily edged his way over to the tree.

Just as Bite was about to pick up the didgeridoo,
the naughty crocodiles spotted him.

"GET BITE!" they shouted,
'snap, snap, snapping'
as they rushed towards him.

Although Bite was the guardian of Kingdom Underwatervania,
the apex predator with very sharp teeth,
he didn't want to hurt anyone.
Bite, of course, was a **VEGETARIAN.**

He quickly reached for the didgeridoo.

UMMMM! UMMMM! UMMMM!!!

Just like magic, the crocodiles
froze mid-stride as Bite played
this beautiful, enchanting music.

Their eyes closed;
their heads felt heavy.

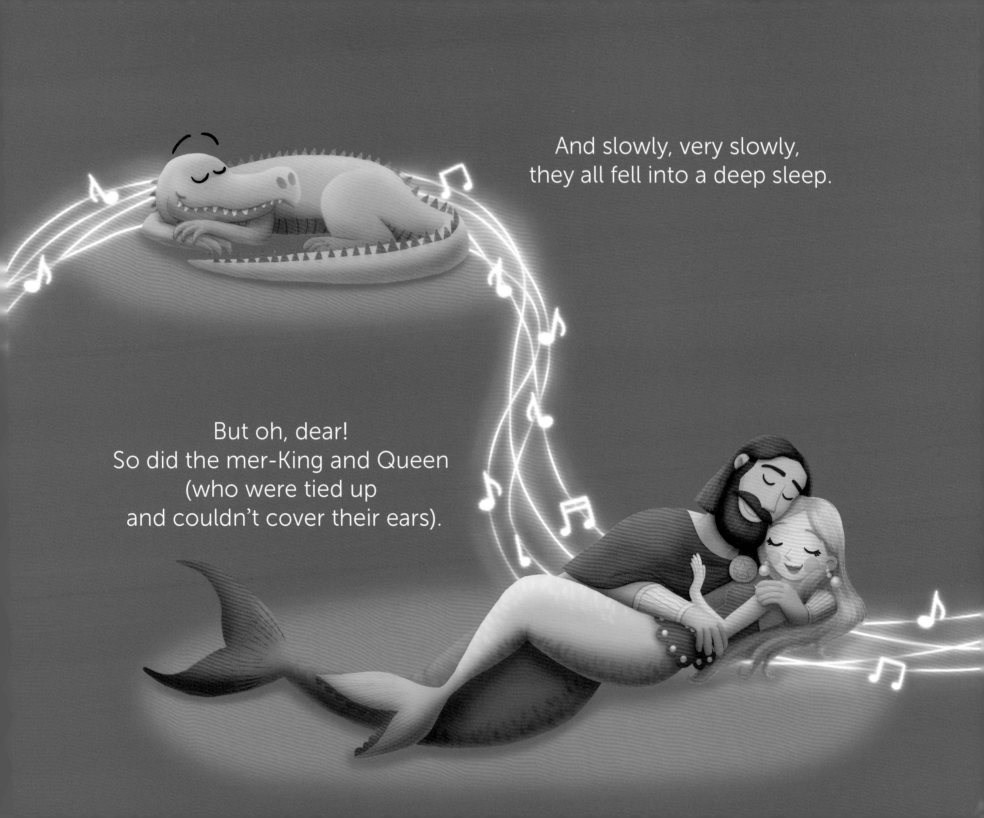

And slowly, very slowly,
they all fell into a deep sleep.

But oh, dear!
So did the mer-King and Queen
(who were tied up
and couldn't cover their ears).

Bite stopped playing.
The SAS guards freed the mer-King and Queen
and carefully carried the sleeping royals and the treasure back to the sea.
Bite considered leaving the magical didgeridoo
but thought it might come in handy one day.

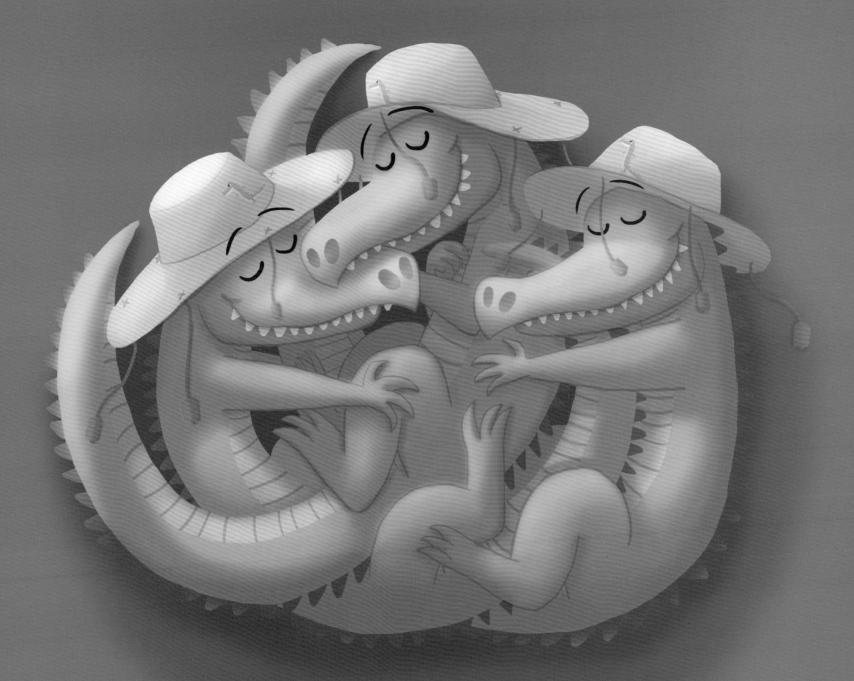

"Just one more thing", he said, pushing all the snoring crocodiles together
as though they were having one **BIG CUDDLE.**
"It's always good to have a bedtime snuggle".

Bite, and his SAS Guards returned
home to a heroes welcome,
complete with loud fanfares
and extremely loud fireworks.

It didn't take long before the bright and colourful lights, crashes and bangs woke up the snoring mer-King and Queen. After the medal presentation, Bite was ready for bed! Unlike everyone else, he hadn't had a chance for a snooze.

At home, he told Mrs Bite all about his adventure.
Just as they wiggled into their pyjamas, they heard THE SOUND.

wweehhehe
wweee snap!

Weeee
weee snap!

Baby Bite.

How Bite the Shark came to life

After Monika read the whole book and talked with Nigel about how he imagined it to look like, she made a rough sketch of every page.

Keeping the drawings loose helps her to focus on the most important elements of this scene.

Can you tell what this scene is telling us about Bite?

Bite doesn't mind being different.
He loves how being a vegetarian makes him strong and healthy.
In fact, he is so strong and healthy that the mer-King and Queen made him
the guardian of Kingdom Underwatervania
(which is a big deal if you live underwater).

When Nigel approved the black and white sketches, Monika designed the colours.

It's very important at the beginning to focus on big shapes and be loose. It helps to quickly change things if something needs to be red instead of blue.

Monika begins to carefully draw all the elements now. She starts with simple shapes and colours, and then draws a few lines to separate the flat shapes.

Without a single line on Bite you could hardly tell where his chin ends and where his proud chest starts.

Finally, Monika adds shadow and light to everything!

The mer-King and Queen's tails sparkle in the light, and Bite proudly protects Underwatervania's castle, while a school of fish swim among the bubbles.

How to draw

1.

2.

3.

4.

5.

6.

7.

8.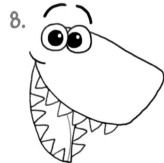

9.

Bite the Shark

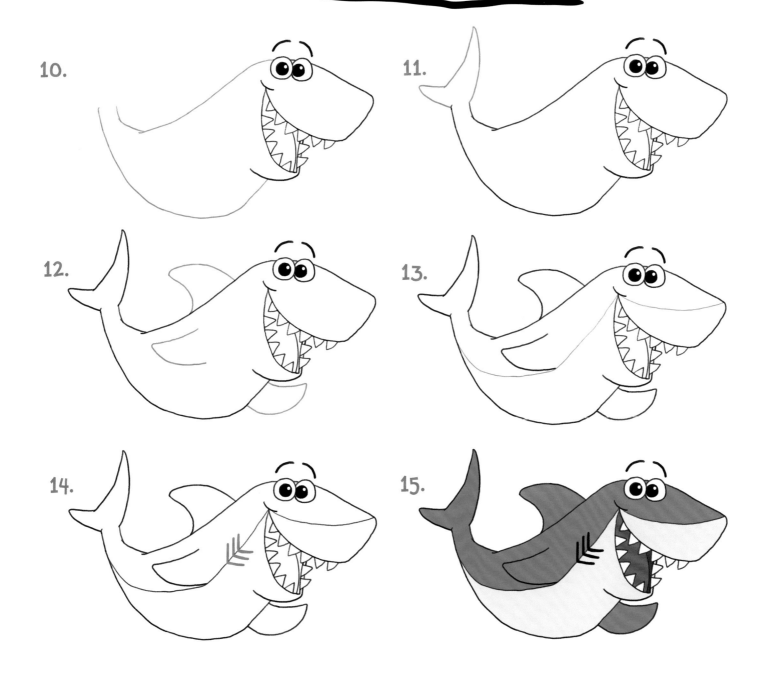

Nigel McGee - Author

Nigel is an English author and Bite The Shark And The Magical Didgeridoo is his first published book.

Bite began life as a bedtime story to his daughter. With her help, its creation has taught him that when you dare to imagine and take bold action, anything is possible. He hopes this book brings enjoyment, inspiration and courage.

Here's to Bite's next adventure!

www.nigelmcgee.com

Monika Dzikowicz - Illustrator

Monika is a Polish illustrator who is passionate about drawing unique and expressive characters.

She is always on a lookout for magical and wonderful things in life, just like Bite's didgeridoo.

However, instead of the didgeridoo she found the magic and wonder in visualising stories, which empower people and bring positive change into their lives.

www.monikadzikowicz.com

To my daughter Evie who is the inspiration and reason. To Max, Louis, Mum & Dad and my wife Linds, with her boundless love, support and joy without who non of this would have been possible. You are my lifeboats!

Nigel McGee

Thank you to my husband for his unsinkable support.
You teach me how to bravely keep swimming forward.

Monika Drikowicz

Bite the Shark
and the magical Sea Unicorn